This dragon book belongs to:

....

Potty Train Your Dragon
My Dragon Books - Volume 1
Written by Steve Herman

ISBN: 978-1-948040-06-8 (paperback)
ISBN: 978-1-948040-25-9 (hardcover)

www.MyDragonBooks.com

First Edition: December 2017

10 9 8 7 6 5 4 3 2 1

Potty Train Your Dragon

My Dragon Books - Volume 1

Steve Herman

Some kids have a dog or two;
some prefer a cat,
Some kids have a guinea pig,
a hamster, or a rat.

Some kids have a lizard,
a snake, or cockatoo –
I have a dragon by the name
of Diggory Doo.

A dragon is not practical;
they take a lot of training.

Like not to sit on furniture,
for they've been known to break it

And not breathe fire when in the house and accidently bake it.

But Diggory Doo was pretty swell
as far as dragons go,
For I had trained him very well in
what dragons ought to know –

Like stay off beds and furniture
and sit upon the floor
And not go belching fire
and smoke whenever he would roar.

And when I would throw a Frisbee,
Diggory Doo could catch it.

When it came to doing tricks, Diggory Doo was able,

And he hardly ever begged beneath the dinner table.

But one important thing that Diggory would not do –

When it was time to potty, Diggory would not poo!

As you know, it's quite important to potty train your pet,

But to potty train a dragon is pretty tough, you bet!

Diggory Doo refused to poo
and strained to hold it in.

Then one day a puff of smoke came from Diggory's "other" end –

I tell you nothing smells quite like a dragon breaking wind!

Then Diggory Doo began
to cry great big dragon tears,
So I pet Diggory on the back
and tried to calm his fears.

He was going poo where
no dragon had ever gone!

Get your FREE Gift from Diggory Doo at
www.MyDragonBooks.com/gift

Read more about Drew and Diggory Doo!

Visit
www.MyDragonBooks.com
for more!